SUPER POTATO

#1 THE EPIC ORIGIN OF SUPER POTATO

ARTUR LAPERLA

Graphic Universe™ • Minneapolis

Story and illustrations by Artur Laperla
Translation coordinated by Graphic Universe™

First American edition published in 2018 by Graphic Universe™

Graphic Universe™
A division of Lerner Publishing Group, Inc.
241 First Avenue North
Minneapolis, MN 55401 USA

For reading levels and more information, look up this title at www.lernerbooks.com.

Main body text set in CCWildWords 8.5/10. Typeface provided by Comicraft.

Library of Congress Cataloging-in-Publication Data

Names: Laperla (Artist) author, illustrator.
Title: The epic origin of Super Potato / Artur Laperla.
Description: First American edition. | Minneapolis : Graphic Universe, 2018. | Series: Super
    Potato ; #1 | Summary: After Doctor Malevolent turns him into a potato, Super Max must
    learn how to fight crime as a vegetable. | Identifiers: LCCN 2017043534 (print) | LCCN
    2017055277 (ebook) | ISBN 9781541523791 (eb pdf) | ISBN 9781512440218 (lb : alk. paper) |
    ISBN 9781541526457 (pb : alk. paper)
Subjects: LCSH: Graphic novels. | CYAC: Superheroes—Fiction. | Potatoes—Fiction. |
    Humorous stories. | Graphic novels.
Classification: LCC PZ7.7.L367 (ebook) | LCC PZ7.7.L367 Ep 2018 (print) | DDC 741.5/973—dc23

LC record available at https://lccn.loc.gov/2017043534

Manufactured in the United States of America
1-42290-26140-11/7/2017

THAT DOCTOR MALEVOLENT IS ALWAYS STEALING THINGS . . .

. . . AND I ALWAYS HAVE TO GO TO HIS SECRET HIDEOUT, THWART HIM, AND RETURN THEM.

SUPER MAX HAS BEEN TO THE DOCTOR'S SECRET HIDEOUT SO MANY TIMES, IT'S NOT MUCH OF A SECRET ANYMORE.

DOESN'T HE GET TIRED OF THIS?

HE HAS TO BREAK DOWN THE DOOR. EVERY SINGLE TIME.

BLAM

6

10

*THE AVERAGE HUMAN BODY ONLY HAS 650 MUSCLES. SUPER MAX HAS 87 MORE.

NORMALLY, SUPER MAX GIVES A FEW LUMPS TO DOCTOR MALEVOLENT AND THAT'S THAT.

EH HEH HEH HEH!
A HA HA HA HA HA!

BUT THIS TIME, OUR HERO HAS LOST THE FIGHT.

A POTATO!

I'M A POTATO!

SUPER MAX HAS NOT CRIED EVEN ONCE IN THE LAST FIFTEEN YEARS.

BUT WHILE SUPER MAX MAY NOT CRY, SUPER *POTATO* CRIES LIKE A BABY SURROUNDED BY ONIONS.

WAAA! WAAA! BWAAAAAAAAA!

FIFTY-SEVEN MINUTES LATER . . .

SNIFF
SNIFF
SNIFF

I GUESS . . .
I GUESS . . .
I SHOULD
HEAD HOME . . .
SNIFF . . .

IF ONLY I COULD STILL FLY . . .

BUT WAIT!
HE HASN'T EVEN TRIED!

BUT SUPER POTATO WILL HAVE TO TRY SOON, BECAUSE...

SIGH. IT'S GOING TO BE A LONG WALK.

...HE HEADS ACROSS THE STREET WITHOUT LOOKING FIRST. WHICH YOU SHOULD NEVER DO, EVEN IF YOU'RE THE WORLD'S SADDEST POTATO.

BRoooooo

BROOOOOOO

AAAH!

BROO

SUPER POTATO IS FURIOUS.

CRASH

I'M BACK, DOCTOR MALEVOLENT!

DOCTOR MALEVOLENT?

WHERE IS HE?

HMM . . .

AFTER RECOVERING, DOCTOR MALEVOLENT DECIDED TO TREAT HIMSELF TO A SUPER DINNER TO CELEBRATE HIS SUPER VICTORY OVER SUPER MAX.

TONIGHT WE'RE DINING AT THE GOLDEN CRAB.

SQUEAK.

I'LL EAT NEXT TO A RAT! I WON'T EVEN WEAR A TIE! THE WORLD WILL DENY ME NOTHING. **NOTHING!**

SO THE EVIL DOCTOR HOPPED IN HIS MALEVOLENT MOBILE, READY FOR A NIGHT OF FINE DINING . . .

EH HEH HEH! *A HA HA HA!*

HE ARRIVED READY TO GOBBLE AT LEAST THREE LOBSTERS AND A PLATTER OF CRAB LEGS.

ANDRE, MY GOOD MAN.

HELLO, MR. MALEVOLENT.

DOCTOR. TABLE FOR A VICTORIOUS SUPERVILLAIN, PLEASE.

FORGIVE ME, BUT I SEE YOU'RE NOT WEARING A TIE. AND THERE'S A SLIGHT ISSUE WITH YOUR—*AHEM*—COMPANION.

OH, NO. AN ISSUE?

23

SUDDENLY, SUPER POTATO CATCHES A GLANCE OF SOMETHING HE HASN'T SEEN YET . . .

AAAH!

HIS REFLECTION!

THIS IS ME!?

NO. NO.

OH, NO! CAN I GET A DO-OVER?

SUPER POTATO LEAVES THE PRICELESS STATUE ON THE NEAREST ROOF.

I CAN'T FACE DOCTOR MALEVOLENT LIKE THIS!

CRASH

WHAT WOULD PEOPLE THINK?

SUPER POTATO HAS RETURNED HOME...

I MUST BE SWIFT. NO TIME TO LOSE!

BUT WHAT IS OUR HERO LOOKING FOR IN THOSE BOXES?

YES! IT'S HERE!

THE DELUXE SUPER MAX ACTION FIGURE!

THE DELUXE SUPER MAX ACTION FIGURE WAS A RARE GIANT DISASTER IN THE SUCCESSFUL CAREER OF SUPER MAX. THE TOY'S HAIRPIECE FELL OFF EASILY, ALARMING MANY CHILDREN AND POSING VARIOUS SAFETY ISSUES.

Official Super Max merchandise!

Movable arms!

DEFECTIVE HAIR!

THE ACTION FIGURE WAS TAKEN OFF THE MARKET AFTER A SERIES OF HAIR-RELATED COMPLAINTS.

Only $19.99!

SUPER POTATO HAS FINALLY FOUND A USE FOR THAT FAULTY HAIRPIECE.

MUCH BETTER!

ALL I NEED NOW IS A CAPE.

SUPER POTATO GETS SO BUSY FIXING HIS LOOK THAT HE FAILS TO NOTICE THE GENERAL'S CALL.

SUPER MAX! WHERE HAVE YOU BEEN?

WHO'S THE HANDSOMEST POTATO OF THEM ALL?

DOCTOR MALEVOLENT IS OUT OF CONTROL! LOOK WHAT HE'S DONE TO ME!

29

33

34

BUT THEY'RE BACK AT WORK BEFORE MORNING.

WAKE UP, MALEVOLENT! YOU HAVE TO FINISH THE BEAM!

JUST A LITTLE MORE SLEEP...

SOON THEY'VE WORKED FOR TWO DAYS, THEN THREE, THEN FOUR, AND THEN NINE FULL DAYS AND NIGHTS...

NOW WHAT ARE YOU MAKING?

A POLYPEPTIDE SYNTHESIZER. PASS ME THE HAMMER.

AND THEN, AT LONG LAST, AFTER 379 HOURS...

IT'S DONE!

LET ME SEE! LET ME SEE!

42

DOCTOR MALEVOLENT, IN HIS QUEST TO FINISH OFF SUPER POTATO . . .

AHA HA HA HA!

. . . DOESN'T SEE THAT HE'S TRASHING HIS OWN LABORATORY.

RRRRR

THAT'S IT, KEEP FOLLOWING ME.

AND THE DOCTOR SHOULD BE CAREFUL AROUND HIS LABORATORY, BECAUSE IF NOT . . .

SODIUM.

CRAS

WATER.

BLA

HOLD ON, HERE'S A SCIENTIST TO EXPLAIN WHAT HAPPENS WHEN SODIUM MIXES WITH WATER.

AS A CHEMICAL ELEMENT, SODIUM IS HIGHLY UNSTABLE, MUCH LIKE CERTAIN PEOPLE IN THIS STORY. ITS REACTION MECHANISM WITH WATER IS $2Na_{(S)} + 2H_2O \rightarrow 2NaOH_{(AQ)} + H_{2(G)}$.

WELL, ANYWAY, THAT MEANS YOU CAN PRODUCE . . .

SUPER POTATO STOPS, DROPS, AND ROLLS TO PUT OUT THE FIRE.

HUFF! HUFF!

WHAT A DISASTER!

BUT . . .

WHERE'S DOCTOR MALEVOLENT?

ONE MONTH LATER...

IN PRISON, DOCTOR MALEVOLENT HAS DISCOVERED HIS TRUE CALLING: GARDENING.

SURE YOU DON'T WANT TO BREAK OUT?

NO, NO, YOU GO. I'M GOOD HERE!

A GROUP OF SCIENTISTS IS TRYING TO CREATE A DE-POTATO-IZING BEAM, WITHOUT MUCH SUCCESS.

SO FAR WE'VE ONLY MANAGED TO TURN A POTATO INTO A CARROT.

HMMM.

AND THINGS IN THE CITY ARE BACK TO NORMAL, MORE OR LESS.

YOUR TURN, ANDRE.

WHAT DO I DO NOW? I'M A POTATO!

SO, BEFORE YOU PICK UP THE NEXT SUPER ADVENTURE OF SUPER POTATO, WE MUST BRING THIS ONE TO A CLOSE.

MIRROR, MIRROR, ON THE WALL. WHO'S THE HANDSOMEST POTATO OF THEM ALL?

SUPER POTATO! BIG JAW AND THE FERRET HAVE ESCAPED FROM PRISON! WE NEED YOUR HELP!

YEP, THAT'S IT! *THE END.*

Available soon:
The second adventure in the Super Potato saga,

SUPER POTATO'S GALACTIC BREAKOUT

TRAPPED—IN AN OUTER SPACE ZOO!

Zort the Third is an alien king with a rude hobby. He zooms through space, capturing new breeds for his collection of rare creatures. He has a Buzzillion from Planet Buzz and a Zazzarina from Planet Zazz. But when he snags Earth's top superhero, he gets more than he bargained for.

Zort's about to learn what happens when you cage a crime fighter. Because no zoo—on Earth or in space—can hold Super Potato. Our hero is planning an escape that will turn the galaxy upside down. It's time for Super Potato to break out!